First published in Great Britain in 2020 by Hodder and Stoughton

Text and illustrations © Rikin Parekh, 2020

HB ISBN: 978 1 44494 156 2 • PB ISBN: 978 1 44494 157 9

10 9 8 7 6 5 4 3 2 1

Printed and bound in China.

Hodder Children's Books
An imprint of Hachette Children's Group
Part of Hodder and Stoughton
Carmelite House, 50 Victoria Embankment, London EC4Y 0DZ

An Hachette UK Company
www.hachette.co.uk
www.hachettechildrens.co.uk

For my greatest teachers, my mother Mina and my father Kirit. Thank you, XX. - R. P.

Fly
TiGER
Fly

RIKIN PAREKH

Riku the Tiger wanted to be something **SPECIAL**.
ALL the tigers in his family had done amazing
things. Their portraits hung proudly on
the Triumphant Tiger Tree.

Ever since he was a tiny cub,
had wanted to be the **FIRST EVER**...

FLYING TIGER.

He dreamt of soaring through the clouds with his best friend, Jim.

Riku's family had always encouraged him.

The sky's the limit, Riku!

Never give up, son. Try, try and try some more!

Only Jim was doubtful.
"**HOW** will you fly?! Tigers don't have wings. **EVERYONE** knows that!"

"Never fear, my little feathered friend," said Riku. "I have a **PLAN!**"

You'll see!

"TA-DA! TIGER WINGS!

Aren't they amazing?"

"TIGER WINGS?" Jim squawked.

"I'm not sure about this, Riku . . ."

"Silence, Jim!" said Riku.

"And prepare to see the world's first ever

FLYING TIGER!

READY....

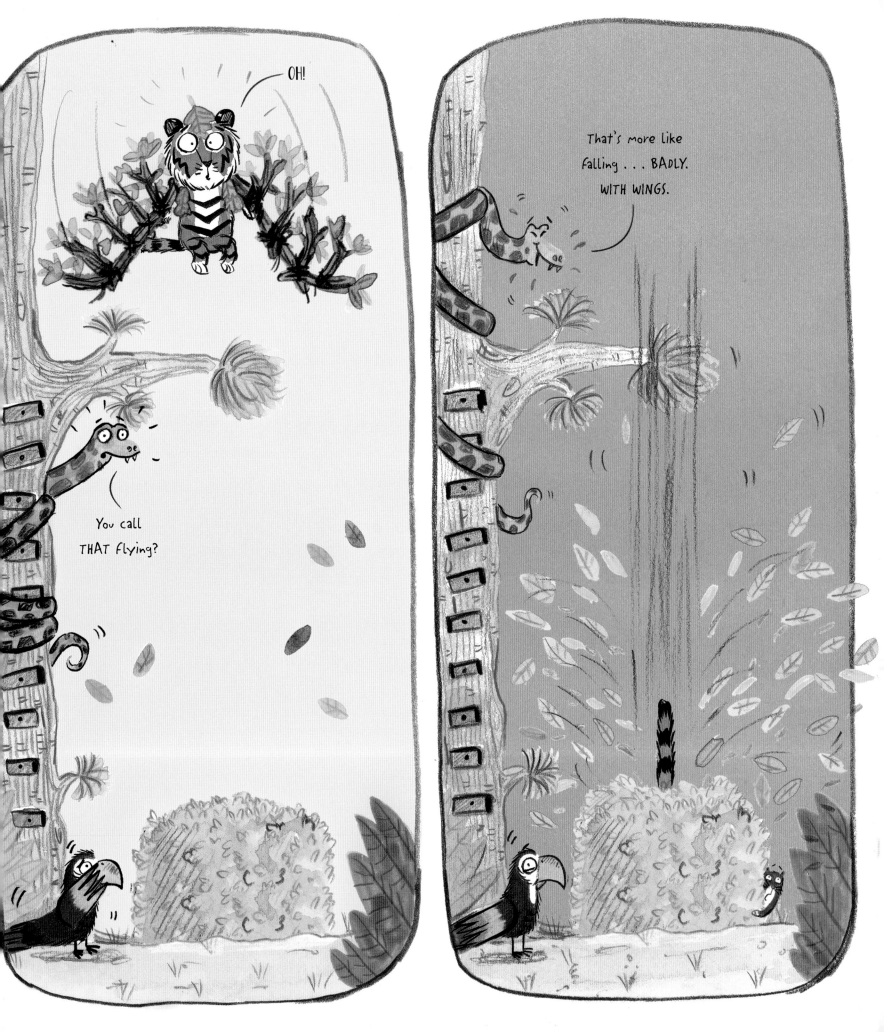

Riku landed with a **THUMP!** at the bottom of the Triumphant Tiger Tree.

"Fear not, my feathered friend," said Riku. "This little tiger never gives up! I **WILL** fly. Come with me to my Tiger Cave . . ."

Oh dear, Riku, that must have hurt!

The walls of Riku's cave were covered in pictures . . . of flying tigers!
"Whoa! You're really passionate about flying, aren't you, Riku?" said Jim.
"These are amazing!"

"C'mon, Jim," said Riku, "let's make me FLY."

Riku and Jim tried . . .

SPRINGS,

BEANS,

AN UMBRELLA JET,

A PROPELLER BEANIE,

A BOUNCY CASTLE

AND BALLOONS.

But **NOTHING** worked.

"I never give up," said Riku. "I still have a trick up my sleeve . . ."

But you don't HAVE any sleeves, Riku!

"Friends, family," said Riku, "behold the **CANNON**-THAT-WILL-MAKE-RIKU-FLY-AND-HE-**WILL**-BECOME-THE-WORLD'S-**FIRST-FLYING**-TIGER." Are you ready, Jim?"

A drum roll, please!

SH!

Lucky you were wearing a helmet, Riku!

As Riku lay in the grass, he felt very silly. **AND** his head hurt. "You were right, Jim," he groaned. "Who was I kidding? I'll never fly, no matter **HOW** hard I try. I'm just a **TIGER** . . .

. . . the world's first ever **COMPLETELY**

USELESS TIGER."

Jim watched as his friend walked away. He wanted to help – but how? Tigers weren't meant to fly. It simply wasn't possible.

And then – **BINGO** – it came to him. "Riku, wait!" cried Jim. **"DON'T GIVE UP!** I've got it. I know what you need to get off the ground."

I don't know why I didn't think of this before!

Quickly, Jim gathered all the birds in the forest: sparrows, toucans, cockatoos and parakeets. He explained his ingenious plan.

"Riku, you **CAN** fly! You just need the help of some Bird Power . . .

"...**AND** this paraglider we've made out of our feathers. Come on, everyone, let's make some **WIND!**"

Hundreds of birds began to FLIP...FLAP...AND

He said wind! Hehehe!

FLUTTER...

UNTIL...

SWOOOOOOSH!

Riku was off the ground.

"This is the most amazing thing **EVER!**"

yelled Riku. "Thank you, Jim! Thank you, birds!

I'M FLYING! I really am FLYING!"

Riku and Jim soared through the skies.
It was just as Riku had dreamt, but a million,
MILLION times better. He wasn't in the
jungle any more, he was **ABOVE IT**.

And there was one very special place Riku wanted to fly to . . .

"**YES!** I'm the first **EVER FLYING TIGER**," said Riku as he hung his portrait with the other great tigers on Triumphant Tiger Tree. "I did it – **WE** did it!"

AUNTY SHINA
FIRST TIGER EVER TO HAVE RAINBOW WHISKERS

UNCLE ROHAN
FIRST TIGER EVER TO BECOME A MAGICIAN

RIKU
FIRST EVER FLYING TIGER!

"Err, Jim," said Riku . . .

". . . just one small question. How exactly am I going to get down?"

Jim smiled. "Riku, my fluffy little friend, **THAT** is a different story altogether!"